Alex 7e gr

D1576198

THE CLASHING ROCKS

To hide him from his wicked uncle King Pelias, Jason is brought up in exile by Chiron the centaur. When Jason returns home determined to overthrow the tyrant King, cunning Pelias tricks him into undertaking an impossible quest. He must journey to the kingdom of Colchis and steal back the Golden Fleece from its keeper – a monstrous serpent who never sleeps. Only then will Pelias give Jason back his crown.

To help him, Jason has the crew of his magic ship the *Argo* including mighty Heracles and Orpheus the musician. Even the goddess Hera lends a hand. But there is also Medea the sorceress. To help Jason she will stop at nothing, even murder. Jason finds himself struggling with magical powers that may yet undo all his plans …

First told over three thousand years ago, the story of Jason is one of the oldest and best loved of the Greek myths.

IAN SERRAILLIER

THE CLASHING ROCKS

JASON AND —THE— ARGONAUTS

Heinemann
New Windmills

Heinemann Educational Publishers
Halley Court, Jordan Hill, Oxford OX2 8EJ
a division of Reed Educational & Professional Publishing Ltd
OXFORD   MELBOURNE   AUCKLAND
JOHANNESBURG   BLANTYRE   GABORONE
IBADAN   PORTSMOUTH (NH) USA   CHICAGO

ISBN 0 435 12147 2

99 00 20 19 18 17 16 15

Illustrated by William Stobbs
Cover illustration by Kevin Jenkins

Printed in England by Clays Ltd, St Ives plc

TO ANTHONY

Acknowledgements

The author is grateful for the valuable help and guidance he has received from the following books:

Trans. Sir J. G. Frazer: Apollodorus (*Heinemann*)

Trans. R. C. Seaton: Apollonius Rhodius (*Heinemann*)

Trans. E. V. Rieu: Apollonius of Rhodes, The Voyage of Argo (*Penguin Books*)

Robert Graves: The Greek Myths (*Penguin Books*)

C. Kerenyi: The Gods of the Greeks (*Penguin Books*)

C. Kerenyi: The Heroes of the Greeks (*Thames and Hudson*)

J. Lemprière: Lemprière's Classical Dictionary (*Routledge and Kegan Paul*)

Ovid, trans. F. J. Miller: Metamorphoses (*Heinemann*)

Rex Warner: Men and Gods (*MacGibbon and Kee*)

Contents

1 THE MOUNTAIN CAVE

One stormy winter day a man was struggling up the wooded slopes of Mount Pelion. In his arms he held a woollen bundle; he hugged it close, to protect it from the bitter wind.

High up, just above the tree-line, he found a cave, and from it came the sound of a harp and a man's voice singing. He knew then that he had come to the right place. Gently he laid the bundle down in the mouth of the cave, out of the wind and the cold, then hurried back down the mountain, across the fields and vineyards, to the palace in Iolcos where he had come from. Though he lived in a palace he was only a servant, but one who had been entrusted with a dangerous and secret task. He returned now to his master to tell him it had been fulfilled.

The singer who lived in the mountain cave was Chiron the centaur, half man and half horse. He soon saw the bundle and picked it up and was astonished when it began to wail and cry. Opening it, he found a baby boy inside. There was also a letter from Aeson, the boy's father, asking Chiron to look after the baby, bring him up wisely and teach him all that a royal prince should know. Aeson was not King of Iolcos,

though he should have been by right. But his half-brother Pelias had seized the throne and made him and his wife Alcimede prisoners in the palace. When a son was born to them they were afraid that Pelias would kill him. So they pretended that the baby had been born dead and gave it to their servant to smuggle out of the city and take to Chiron.

Aeson knew that Chiron had other children in his care, sons of heroes and princes, who afterwards won great fame. The wise and gentle centaur looked after them all; in music, medicine and archery there was no greater teacher anywhere. And he gave the boy the name of Jason.

At first the mountain nymphs helped him, for he

was not used to babies. But when Jason was six Chiron looked after him alone, loving him as if he had been his own son and teaching him all his skills. He taught him medicine and the use of herbs, many of which he grew in a sheltered plot outside the cave and which he gave now to Jason to tend. He taught him to read and write and draw, to play the lyre and the harp, to hunt the deer and the wild goats. He encouraged him to be brave and self-reliant. Jason might not be as strong as Heracles, as resourceful as Aeneas, both older boys than he, but he could stand the winter snows and the scorching summer sun as well as they. He had also great nobility and charm, and in poetry and music, which woke the gentleness in his nature, he far excelled all his friends. As they grew to manhood, one by one they left Chiron, but there were always others to take their place.

At last the time came for Jason to consider what he should do with his life. Chiron advised him to consult the oracle.

'Go back to Iolcos,' the oracle replied. 'Pelias has no right to the throne, and you must claim it for your father Aeson, the rightful king.'

So Jason got ready to leave. He put on a leather tunic and a leopard-skin to keep off the rain and armed himself with a sword and spear. Then he said good-bye to Chiron.

'Today I shall give my father back his throne,' he

said, speaking more bravely than he felt, for the sadness of parting had almost overwhelmed him.

'Be patient, Jason. You have many dangers to face yet,' said Chiron. 'But you are strong in spirit and I have told you how to meet them.'

Jason looked out over the hills and the forests and the great plain of Thessaly which stretched far into the blue distance. Suddenly he felt very lonely. 'Dear Chiron,' he cried, 'I shall never again have your wisdom to guide me. There is no one as wise as you.'

'Do you think me as wise as the gods?' Chiron laughed. 'If you can believe that, then I have taught you nothing. However, since you value my words so much, I will advise you for today. Remember two things—treat courteously anyone you meet, and keep your word. Go safely, my son, and with my blessing.'

Jason kissed the centaur's hand and thanked him from his heart. And they parted.

2 THE CROSSING OF THE TORRENT

Jason ran down the wooded slopes of the mountain until he came to a torrent which blocked his path. It was springtime and the snows were melting. The water was in full spate, spilling from the lips of tall rocks, thundering through gorges and pounding its white way past cliffs and boulders down towards the plain. He looked for a place to cross and was about to plunge in and let the current carry him to a midstream boulder, when he heard a shout behind him.

An old hag was standing on a rock above his head, waving her stick at him and crying out, 'Boy! Carry me to the other bank!'

Jason looked up at her, then down at the swirling water, and he shuddered. With her weight on his back, how could he hope to get across? If he missed the boulder they would both be swept over the fall and dashed to pieces on the rocks below.

'Hurry, hurry!' she screamed. 'The water's rising all the time—we cannot wait. In the name of the goddess Hera, carry me across!'

Jason might have refused, but he remembered Chiron's parting words.

'I'll take you for Hera's sake!' he called up to her. 'But I must find a safer place to cross.'

'I cannot wait, I cannot wait!' she screamed. And she flung away her stick and with one long leap landed on Jason's back. He was knocked into the stream, with her skinny yellow hands half choking him and her bony knees digging into his ribs.

His mouth was under water and he felt the current whisk up his legs. He kicked with his feet, he clawed at the water—and grabbed for the midstream boulder. The current was so strong that it curled his legs right round it and forced back his chin; but he clung on with his fingers and with an effort hauled himself up with the dragging weight on his back, then lay on top, panting for breath.

'You've soaked me to the skin!' the old woman cried. 'Hurry on before I die of cold.'

He staggered to his feet, longing to shrug off the wet burden from his back. But there was a white roaring channel between him and the next boulder and he must leap it. She rode him like a jockey and spurred him to the jump with her sharp heels. Over he went and landed and by a miracle held his balance. There was quieter water beyond, and he waded through it waist-deep to the shore.

'Some god must have helped me,' said Jason as he set down his wet bundle.

He spat out the water from his lungs and turned to

the old hag. But she had vanished and in her place stood a lady of surpassing beauty.

'I am the goddess Hera, the wife of Zeus,' she said, smiling at him. 'You helped me when I needed you. If ever you want my help, call me and I shall be there.'

She sprang into the air and floated through the mist

of spray that hung above the trees, away to her golden throne on Mount Olympus.

Jason wrung the water from his tunic and his leopard-skin. He still had his sword and spear, but he had lost a sandal in the torrent. And he walked on to Iolcos, with one foot shod and the other bare.

3 A CRUEL KING

When Jason arrived in the market-place of Iolcos, he found it crowded with people all waiting for King Pelias to come and sacrifice to the gods. Pheres and Admetus, two kings from neighbouring cities, were sitting on the stone bench near the priests. But the crowd were staring at Jason and trying to guess who he could be. Some thought he was Apollo, the god of voyages, of music and poetry; others thought he must be Ares, the god of war.

A mule carriage drew up and King Pelias stepped out. When he saw the handsome young stranger and noticed that he was wearing only one sandal he was suddenly afraid. An oracle had once warned him that a man with one sandal would steal his kingdom and cause his death. Hiding his fear, he called the young man to him and asked him who he was and what was his father's name.

Jason answered frankly, for he did not realize that he was talking to King Pelias himself.

'But Aeson has no son,' said Pelias.

When Jason told him how he had been smuggled out of the palace and brought up by Chiron, Pelias grew more and more uneasy. But because of the two kings he dared not lay hands on him. If Jason's words were true, then the kings were Jason's uncles by marriage and would take his side.

'And what is your business with Aeson?' said Pelias.

'To claim the throne of Iolcos for him. It is his by right—Pelias usurped it.'

There was a gasp from the crowd and much murmuring against Pelias, who was a harsh and hated ruler. A less cunning man would have called his guard and arrested Jason. But Pelias only smiled and said, 'Suppose an oracle had told you that one of your fellow citizens was destined to murder you. What would you do?'

'I would send him on some desperate errand from which he would not return,' said Jason. 'He should go to Colchis to fetch the Golden Fleece.'

'And if the destined murderer were yourself? Would you still go?'

'Of course,' said Jason. 'If I could bring back the Fleece, I would avenge the death of my relative Phrixus and prove my manhood, too.'

'Then go and bring it back.'

When Pelias revealed who he was, and that Jason was destined to kill him, the young man saw that he had been trapped. But he did not flinch.

'Sir, you stole my father's birthright,' he said. 'Keep the land and herds you took from him, but give him back his throne.'

'He is too old and feeble to be king.'

'If that is true, then the throne is mine, not yours.'

Pelias was now afraid to deny Jason his birthright, particularly when Pheres and Admetus added their support and urged him to accept the terms. So he agreed, but added cunningly that Jason must first go to fetch the Golden Fleece as he had promised, and so prove that he was fit to be king. 'The oracle has said that our city will not prosper until the Golden Fleece is brought home and the soul of Phrixus is at rest. I would go myself, but I am too old.'

Now Jason already knew the story of Phrixus and the Golden Fleece, for it was one that Chiron had often told him. Years ago when his kinsman Phrixus was still a child, he and his young sister Helle were to have been killed and sacrificed. But a ram with a golden fleece rescued them and carried them off over land and sea. The girl grew tired on the way and fell into the sea, which is still called the Hellespont after her. But Phrixus arrived safely at Colchis, a city at the far end of the Black Sea, where Aietes was King. In gratitude to the gods for his escape, Phrixus sacrificed the ram; but the Golden Fleece was a treasure of rare beauty and he kept it. Aietes wanted it for himself, so he treacherously murdered Phrixus and refused to bury him. Then he hung the Fleece on a tree in a sacred grove and had it guarded night and day by a serpent that never slept.

Jason did not stay to take part in the sacrifice, but

went off in search of his father and mother. He found them living in a wretched hovel hardly fit for pigs, for Pelias had thrown them out of the palace long ago.

How happy they were to be reunited with him, and how distressed was Jason at their plight! In return for his promise to recover the Golden Fleece, he made Pelias give them a house suited to their age and rank. And here he stayed with them both till it was time for the great adventure to begin.

4 THE BUILDING OF THE SHIP

Jason told Argus the shipwright to build a fifty-oared galley strong enough to stand up to a voyage far into the east where no Greek ship had ever sailed before. And the work was started at once.

The tallest pines on Mount Pelion were felled and lopped, then dragged with chains and horses down to the shore. After a good soaking in salt water, they were dried out and cut into lengths. Then Argus and his workmen laid down the keel and attached the stem and stern-post. They shaped the wooden ribs with steam, then fixed planks lengthwise along the hull, overlapping each other, from gunwale to keel. Copper bolts were used for fixing them to the ribs, and the joins were sealed with pitch. They painted the prow vermilion and set into it a beam cut from the oak woods of Dodona. This was a gift from the goddess Athene; it had a human voice and could speak like an oracle. Lastly they made the mast and rowing-benches and fitted the ship with tackle and cordage. And they named her *Argo*, after her builder.

Meanwhile Jason had sent heralds to every court in Greece to find volunteers to go with him. By the time *Argo* was ready for launching, fifty young men and heroes had arrived in Iolcos, bringing with them coats of mail, shields lined with ox-hide, swords of bronze and spears of ashwood, and brass helmets with dyed horse-hair plumes. They were known as the Argonauts, and never before had Iolcos seen so brave and brilliant a company. Among them were Zetes and Calais, the sons of the North Wind, who had wings on their backs and could soar into the sky, their black hair streaming behind them. Another was the Thracian poet Orpheus, who could tame birds, beasts and fishes with his song. There was the great Heracles, one of Chiron's pupils. His strength was superhuman— as a baby he had strangled two serpents that had attacked him. He brought his lion-skin and his famous club, while Hylas, his young page, carried his bow and arrows.

Everyone wanted Heracles to lead the expedition, but he unselfishly refused the honour, saying that the man who had planned it should be the leader. So Jason was chosen.

It was now time to launch the ship, and they dug a runway to the sea and laid down rollers for her to slide on. They placed the oars on board with the blades facing inwards and the handles sticking out through the thole-pins, so that each oarsman could stand by his handle and push. Then Tiphys the helmsman went on board to shout directions. Pushing all together at each shout, they eased her on to the rollers, and soon she

was sliding swiftly through two lines of cheering men. The rollers groaned as the keel scraped over them. Her prow splashed into the sea, and away she ran into the rippling water till the hawsers checked her.

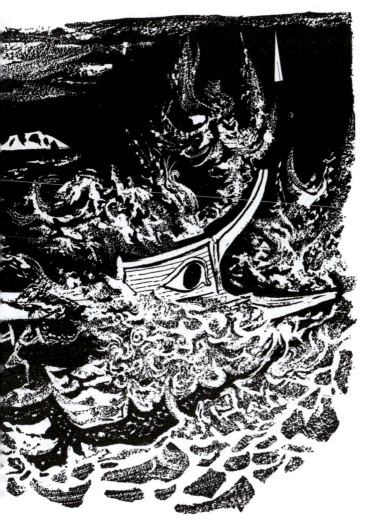

When they had pulled her to the jetty they fixed
the mast and put the sail on board, together with all
the food and water they could carry. Then they made

an altar on the beach and sacrificed two oxen to Apollo.

Among those who had come down to the shore to watch the sacrifice was Jason's mother, Alcimede; his father had been too ill to come. The thought of parting from her son distressed her, but Jason tried to soothe her fears.

'If the gods mean me to die, no tears of yours can save me,' he said. 'But the omens are good. The goddess Hera has promised to help; so have Athene and Apollo. And with such a noble company to sail with me, how can I fail? So be comforted, mother, and forget your distress.'

Yet in spite of his brave words Jason, too, was sad, and his heart went out to the mother he had waited twenty years to see. He kissed her tenderly and hurried back to his friends.

Then Orpheus picked up his lyre and began to sing, and the Argonauts gathered round. He sang of love, the creator of the world, of the birth of the sun and the moon and stars; of the mountains, the murmuring rivers and the wind-whipped sea. And when at last his voice was silent no one spoke or moved. Caught in the spell of his music, they could still hear it ringing in their hearts. And Jason forgot his sadness.

Meanwhile the shadows of the cliffs had lengthened, and the sun had set. And they lay down on the sand and went to sleep.

5 NIGHT LANDING

They were roused at dawn by a cry from the speaking prow. It was *Argo* herself calling, impatient to be off. The sun glanced on the summit of Mount Pelion, and the wave-lashed headlands stood out sharp and clear.

They sat down to their oars, two men to each bench. Because of his huge size Heracles took his place amidships with his club beside him; the keel sank deep into the water under his weight. Tiphys gave the order to cast off the hawsers. Then Orpheus stood at the prow beside Jason, and the fifty oarsmen struck the water together in time to the music of his lyre. Wherever the blades struck, the sea broke into foam and a long white wake trailed behind them.

A huge crowd had gathered on the shore to see them go. Among them was Chiron, who had come down from his cave on Pelion. He waded far out into the water, carrying the little boy Achilles, whose father was on board and had left him in his care. The centaur held him up high so that his father could see him. And the gods in heaven looked down on *Argo*. They could see Jason wearing the crimson cloak that Athene had given him, and in the sunlight all the armour on the ship flashed like fire.

Meanwhile, Tiphys the helmsman stood at the steering-oar. When they were well clear of the shore he ordered the oarsmen to stop rowing. Then they stepped the mast in its box, fixing it with forestays, and hauled up the sail and unfurled it. The wind quickly filled it and *Argo* sped on out of the gulf and into the open sea. It was much rougher here, and as the wind freshened she plunged up and down in the

waves. Then Orpheus took up his lyre and sang a song in honour of the gods. Fish rose out of the sea to listen, sporting and dancing in the wake.

Late in the afternoon, as the wind turned against them and the seas were running high, they beached the ship on the mainland. Here they remained for three days until the storm had blown itself out. Then they turned north up the long Magnesian coast, and when they saw in the distance the cloud-capped summit of Mount Olympus, they turned east across the open sea. After resting on the island of Lemnos, they made straight for the Hellespont and sailed between her narrow shores into the Sea of Marmara.

Finding that they needed to replace their anchor-stone with a heavier one, they put in to the harbour of Fairhaven. Here they were welcomed by Cyzicus, King of the Dolions, a young man of Jason's age, and his bride Cleite, whom he had married that very morning. An oracle had told him to expect the Argonauts and to help them in any way he could. He allowed them to make an altar on the beach for Apollo and gave them the wine and sheep they needed for a sacrifice. Afterwards he invited them to dinner and answered all their questions about what lay beyond. He knew the Sea of Marmara well, but could not tell them anything about the Black Sea, as he had never been so far.

Next morning they set off again and sailed to the east. Towards dusk the wind freshened to a gale and drove them back the same way as they had come. In the middle of the night they found themselves drifting towards a dark shore. Jason decided to land, and they hastily made fast the ship's hawsers to a rock. No one realized that this was the same island they had left that morning. In the thick darkness the Dolions mistook them for pirates and attacked, but they were no match for the Argonauts. Cyzicus and seven of his finest soldiers were killed, and the rest fled in panic. It was not till daylight that both sides realized the ghastly mistake. When he saw the body of his kind host lying in the dust Jason was heartbroken. They laid Cyzicus in his tomb and then heaped on it a great mound that could be seen far out at sea. And they mourned for three days. Then, after the custom of the times, they held funeral games in his honour. Unable to face life without him, Cleite his young bride died of grief. The woodland nymphs mourned her and their tears turned into a fountain of clear water.

6 THE CRY IN THE DARK

There was not a breath of wind when they rowed away. As it was useless to put up the sail, they decided to have a rowing contest to see who could last out longest at the oar.

Away sped the ship—not even the wind-swift horses of Poseidon the sea-god could have raced her. In the afternoon a wind blew up and the sea turned rough. By now most of the crew were exhausted. One by one they gave up and shipped their oars, till only Jason and Heracles, sitting on opposite sides of the ship, were left. Jason was looking pale and tired, but Heracles with his huge muscular arms was still pulling lustily. At each tug of his oar *Argo* shuddered from stem to stern. As they passed the shoals off Cape Poseidon and reached the mouth of the River Cios in Mysia, Jason fainted and drooped forward. Heracles lasted two more strokes—then his oar broke in half. The blade was swept away in the choppy sea, while Heracles fell backwards off his bench with the other end in his hand. Everyone roared with laughter until he sat up and silenced them with a glare.

'I hate being idle,' he said. 'We must land at once so that I can make myself another oar.' And he tossed the broken end into the sea. Then he noticed Jason slumped over his oar and in his concern for him forgot his own anger. He dipped Jason's helmet in the sea and revived him with the salt water. Everyone was glad to see the blood return to their leader's cheeks, and glad, too, that Heracles had recovered his usual good humour, for his temper—like everything about him— was of giant size.

They anchored at the river mouth and landed, and the inhabitants received them kindly, presenting them with all the sheep and wine they needed. Some of the Argonauts went off to find wood to make a fire; some collected leaves for mattresses to sleep on, and others prepared the evening meal.

Heracles vanished into the forest to look for a tree that he could shape into an oar. He soon found a young pine which was about the right length and had not too many branches. He laid down his bow and quiver, took off his lion-skin and started to batter the roots with his club. When he had loosened them enough, he bent down with one shoulder against the trunk. Gripping it with both hands just above the ground he wrenched it out. Up it came, the mop of untidy roots showering his face with earth. It was like a ship's mast ripped out in a gale, with bits of rope and cordage still trailing from it. The tree would make a splendid oar. He picked up his gear and turned back towards the ship, dragging the tree behind him.

Meanwhile Hylas, his young page, had wandered
off alone with a bronze jug to fetch water for the meal.
He was a good servant and wanted to have everything
ready for his master's return. It was dark now, but the
moon was up and he could see a rough track winding
through the trees. He came to a pool all curtained
round with willows and wild apple trees, whose laden
branches leaned out over the sparkling water. As he
stooped to dip his jug, he saw first the moon's reflection, then a girl's hand and face. He dropped the jug
and cried out in surprise. The nymph of the spring was
peering up at him. She had seen his face under the
silver apples, and it seemed to her that not even a god
could be more beautiful. She clasped his neck with
both hands and drew him down deep into the pool.
Silently the water closed above them, and the pool
was still.

The only Argonaut to hear the page cry out was
Polyphemus, who was out searching for Heracles.
But when he reached the pool there was no sign
of Hylas except for the bronze jug lying in the
reeds.

'Hylas!' he cried. 'Where are you?'

There was no answer.

He drew his sword and searched the bushes in case
some animal had attacked him. Hearing a far-off
crackle of branches, he ran along the path towards it,
waving his sword. But the monster he was expecting

to meet was only Heracles, dragging the tree behind him on his way back to the ship.

When he heard that Hylas had disappeared he was

frantic with anxiety, for he loved him like a son. Throwing down the tree, he snatched the jug and plunged headlong into the wood.

'Hylas! Where are you?' he cried, as he trampled down the thickets. 'Hylas!'

'Hylas!' echoed the dark forest.

Meanwhile the Argonauts had finished their meal and were asleep. They had not noticed the disappearance of their friends. Only Tiphys the helmsman was awake; he was sitting on the shore, waiting for a fair wind. As the morning star rose above the mountains the wind began to blow fresh and strong from the east. It might be days before they had another chance like this. Although it was still dark, he woke the Argonauts and, half asleep as they were, hurried them on board. Quickly they pulled up the anchor-stones and hauled in the ropes astern. As they unfurled the sail it caught the full force of the wind and they were swept out into the deep water, well clear of the line of silver foam that marked the dangerous shoals. And they all blessed Tiphys for his skill.

By now Heracles had reached the far edge of the forest, where the trees were thinner and the mountains began. He had run a long way, and the sweat was streaming from his forehead.

'Hylas! Where are you?' he cried. 'Hylas! Hylas!'

'Hylas!' echoed the mountains.

Out at sea Jason heard the cry, and he thought it was a night bird.

And *Argo* in the moonlight sped on across the furrowed sea.

7 PHINEUS AND THE HARPIES

The sun had risen and the Argonauts were well out to sea before they noticed that three of their number were missing. Some were for going back to fetch them, but Tiphys said that the wind and current were against them and they would be wrecked on the shoals. Then a messenger of Nereus the sea-god spoke to Jason from the waves and told him that it was the will of the gods that the three men should remain behind. So *Argo* sailed on.

Next day they came to an island and landed in a sheltered bay. The King of the island was Amycus, the biggest bully in the world. He used to challenge strangers to a boxing match, and if they refused he threw them over a cliff into the sea. Of those who fought him, few escaped his upper cuts alive.

He appeared now on the beach and refused to let Jason water the ship until one of his crew had fought him.

The best boxer was Pollux. He stepped forward at once and put on the rawhide gloves which Amycus gave him. As they put up their fists he noticed that the King's gloves were studded with brass spikes, but this did not dismay him. Amycus charged like a wild bull, grinding his teeth and whirling his arms. Pollux was quicker on his feet and manoeuvred him round till the sun was in his eyes, then knocked him out with a left hook to the temple.

Then he filled a helmet with water, which he emptied into the fallen champion's face. After a few moments Amycus opened his eyes and blinked, and Pollux made him swear never to bully strangers again. And he took off the King's spiked gloves and threw them into the sea.

Their next port of call was in Eastern Thrace near the mouth of the Bosporus, where Phineus was King. He had been born with the gift of prophecy, but because he had used it to foretell the future Zeus had made him blind, old before his time, and unable to enjoy his food. As soon as he sat down to a meal three creatures called Harpies—they had women's faces, and the bodies, wings and claws of vultures —swooped down from the clouds on to his table. They knocked over the wine and snatched the food, stuffing themselves till they could hold no more.

Phineus was delighted to hear of the Argonauts' arrival, for Zeus had told him that they would rid him of the Harpies. Pale, hollow-cheeked and trembling, he got up from his bed and went to greet them, groping his way along with a stick. His withered body was crusted with dirt, and only the skin seemed to hold his bones together. As he reached the steps to the courtyard he fainted.

Jason caught him as he fell and helped him to a seat, while the Argonauts gathered round, anxious to help.

'I knew you by your hands, Jason,' he said, 'the hands that Peleus hopes will never claim the Golden Fleece. You have a stern task before you.'

'We have come to you, sir, to hear what dangers lie ahead and how to meet them,' said Jason.

'I will tell you all I can. But first I need your help. It is the wish of Zeus that two of your noble company should rid me of the Harpies.' The Argonauts looked puzzled, and he added, 'They will know in good time who they are.' Then he invited them to dinner in the great hall, and they all sat down to eat.

Phineus had hardly lifted the first morsel to his lips, when the screeching Harpies swooped down on him from nowhere and snatched it.

At once Calais and Zetes, the winged sons of the North Wind, drew their swords and sprang into the air. They chased the Harpies out of the palace and over the sea, trying to slash at them with their swords. Over the Floating Isles they caught up with them and would have killed them, had not Iris, the goddess of the rainbow, suddenly appeared and stopped them.

'You may not kill the Harpies, for they belong to Zeus,' she said, while the two brothers hovered in the

air. 'But I promise they will never molest Phineus again.'

Then she banished the foul creatures to their cave in Crete, and away they sped on their wicked wings, gurgling with joy at their escape.

The two brothers flew back to the palace, where they found a fresh meal had been prepared. Phineus, feeling all the better for a bath, thanked them heartily for what they had done, and they all sat down together to enjoy their food. And no one enjoyed it more than he. Free of the Harpies at last, he relished every bite.

Afterwards he gathered his guests round the hearth and, when a slave had heaped logs on the fire, told them of the dangers that lay ahead.

'At the far end of the Bosporus you will see two floating rocks. They guard the entrance to the Black Sea and are called the Clashing Rocks because they clash together with the noise of thunder. Every ship that has tried to sail between them has been crushed to powder, but if you listen to my advice you, my brave friends, may be the first to pass through safely. Take a dove with you and, when you come to the Rocks, set it free. If they clash together and destroy it, you must turn back. But if it flies through unhurt, you may take it as a sign that the gods are friendly and will let you pass.'

He spoke of other dangers, too, but of those that awaited Jason in Colchis he would say nothing, for the gods had sealed his lips. 'Trust the gods and serve them well, and they may help you as they have helped me today. They have been generous indeed.'

'I wish they could have given you back your sight,' said Jason.

'There is no hope of that—both eyes are ruined,' said Phineus. 'But no man should expect more than his share of good fortune, and I have more reason than most to be content.'

They were still talking when the first light of dawn crept into the sky and the daily crowd of visitors began to arrive. Phineus treated them with his usual courtesy and kindness, doing all he could to help them and relieve distress. He was both the leader and the servant of his people, selfless and devoted, as every king should be.

8 THE CLASHING ROCKS

As the Argonauts fought their way up the Bosporus the wind was icy cold and the current, swollen from the melting of frozen rivers in the north, was running against them. Soon they reached the narrowest part of the straits, with lofty cliffs on either side and a mill-race of water rushing between. They could hear far ahead of them the noise of thunder growing louder and louder every minute. As they rounded a bend they glanced over their shoulders and saw great waterspouts being sucked into the sky, and beyond them under a crown of mist two Rocks of steely blue. The Rocks were moving all the time, now clashing together, now drifting apart, then clashing together again while the surf roared and thundered. As the ship came nearer, the noise was deafening. Huge fragments of rock kept breaking off and crashing down, while under the crags the sea had tunnelled out gaping caverns which bellowed and roared as the waves came surging in.

Jason stood at the prow with a white dove in his hand, nervously stroking its feathers. When the moment came, with a prayer on his lips he let it go; he watched it fly through the misty spray, carrying on its fragile wings all their hope. The Rocks opened. It flew straight as an arrow between them. As they moved inwards and clashed together again, a tremendous wave struck them and soared into the sky. The bird was hidden in the spray and mist, and it seemed to the anxious watchers that it had been trapped and crushed. Then the backwash from the falling wave caught *Argo* and sent her spinning and reeling, and it was all Tiphys could do to keep her afloat. As the spray subsided he steadied her. The Rocks had opened again. But the bird was safely through, untouched save for a tail-feather which had been nipped off as the Rocks closed together and was now fluttering down. The Argonauts shouted in triumph, and the bird flew on across the unknown sea.

Then Tiphys cried, 'Let the dove be our pilot, let us follow her!'

They heaved, and oars bent like bows. Tiphys, his eyes on the sea beyond, leaned on the helm and steered for the opening, and the sea sucked the ship in. She trembled from end to end, her timbers groaned and shook. High above them the lurching, nodding, grinding crags hung over them, squeezing out the sky and threatening them with death. The Argonauts ducked their heads in panic, crouched over their oars and struck again and again and again. But the power of the gods was in their arms and guiding the helmsman's hand. The wave slid smoothly under the keel.

The Rocks clashed together—they caught the tip of the rudder and crunched it to powder—but *Argo* was clear, afloat on a gentle sea.

The Argonauts shipped their oars and hugged each other and shouted for joy. Glancing behind them they saw to their amazement that the Rocks, which had never before allowed any ship to pass, now stood apart, one on either side of the straits, rooted in the sea as they stand today.

Then they glanced in front and saw the endless unknown sea that stretched ahead. It was very still, and a gentle music possessed it—the music of harp and voice. All this time Orpheus had been singing, unheard. Now wind and wave were hushed. The gulls had flown down from their nesting places and perched on the mast and rigging to listen. The fish in the sea were listening. The Argonauts were listening. Their fears had been stilled, and all the world seemed to be at peace.

They returned to their oars and rowed tirelessly, a day and a night together, over the friendless sea. At dawn they passed a headland crowned with plane trees, with waves snarling below. On the landward side, half hidden by overhanging trees, was the Cavern of Hades, whose icy breath, puffed each morning from the Underworld, covered rocks and trees with sparkling frost till the midday sun melted it away. Nearby was the mouth of Acheron, river of Hades, spilling from the mountain-side in waterfalls down to the sea.

That same day Tiphys the helmsman was taken ill, and they went ashore to look for herbs to cure him. But they could find nothing suitable and in two days he was dead. This was a shock and disaster that affected them all, for he was the only trained pilot among them. When Ancaeus shyly offered to take his place they accepted, and to everyone's relief he proved a success. In no time *Argo* was speeding along the coast like a gull gliding on the wind.

Soon after they passed the land of the Amazons, the tribe of warrior women, the wind dropped and they had to take to their oars. A day's rowing brought them to the Isle of Ares, the war-god. They were a mile or two from the shore when suddenly one of the rowers cried out in pain and dropped his oar. Jason found a feathered dart in his left shoulder and, looking up, saw a bird as big as a swan circle overhead and fly back to the island. As he dressed the wound he remembered that Phineus had spoken of a flock of birds nesting on the island; they had feathered darts in their wings and attacked strangers.

Another bird dived at them, but Clytius brought it down with an arrow and it flopped into the sea. Then suddenly a flock of many thousands rose from the island and headed towards them. They darkened the sky like a thunder cloud, and their huge shadow trailed across the sea.

Against such numbers fifty bowmen would be little use, and they had no rattles to frighten them away.

The birds were more than half-way across before Jason gave his orders. 'Put on your helmets,' he said. 'Let half the crew keep rowing, one man to each bench. The rest of you, lock your shields together to make a roof. And when I raise my hand, shout with all your lungs.'

The flash of the sun from the helmets, the waving purple crests and the chorus of shouting startled the birds; they screeched and flapped their wings in panic. Some collided with a clang and fell with broken

wings into the sea. The rest let fly their feathered darts
and fled. And the darts fell on the shields like hail-
storms on a roof and bounced harmlessly off.

At last they came in sight of the mountains of the
Caucasus at the far end of the Black Sea. Here the
keen-eyed Lynceus noticed an eagle flying overhead
—the eagle that Zeus sent daily to tear at the heart of

the Titan Prometheus. As a punishment for stealing fire from heaven and giving it to men, he had been chained to the highest peak. The day of his deliverance had not yet arrived.

A few hours later they reached the mouth of the River Phasis, which led to Colchis, their destination. It was nightfall and, lowering sail and mast, they rowed swiftly up the muddy waters, while Jason prayed silently to the goddess Hera. They hid *Argo* in the reeds outside the city, then lay down on deck and waited for dawn.

10 KING AIETES

At sunrise Jason held a council on board. He proposed that they should all stay quietly on the ship, while Telamon and Augeias went with him to the palace of King Aietes. 'I want to see if I can win him over without using force,' he said. 'But you must be ready to defend yourselves if he attacks.'

The plan met with approval, and away he went with his two companions, each of them armed as a precaution. So that they could walk through the city unseen, Hera wrapped them in a mist, which lifted as they reached the palace gates. No one stopped them as they crossed the palace courtyard, and they were able to admire the gay vine trees and the four bubbling fountains. The fountains were the work of Hephaistos, the master-smith. One flowed with wine, another with milk, another with sweet-smelling oil, and the fourth with water that was warm in the evening and in the morning icy cold.

They came to an inner courtyard, flanked on three sides with tall buildings supported by columns. In the largest lived King Aietes and his Queen; in the second his young son Apsyrtus, and in the third his daughter Medea and her maids. Medea worshipped Hecate, the goddess of witchcraft, and in the morning was usually busy in her temple. But today she was at home. When she saw the strangers she gave a little cry, covered her face with a veil, and ran out into the courtyard, followed by her maids. Everyone stopped what he was doing to come and stare at the strangers.

Then King Aietes arrived. Everything about him—his golden robes, his jewelled crown, his sceptre of glittering diamonds—proclaimed that he was the son

of Helios the sun-god. The moment he appeared the servants hurried back to their work—whether it was chopping firewood, heating bath water, or carving up a bull's carcass—for he could not bear to see anyone idle. Then he strode up to the three strangers and said rudely, 'What are you doing here? Do you think we are afraid of invaders?'

'Sir, we have not come to fight or plunder,' said Jason. 'We are Greeks—'

At that word the King's face darkened, for he had been told that no Greeks could ever enter the Black Sea.

'We are from Iolcos,' continued Jason, 'and come in friendship to ask for the Golden Fleece, which is ours by right. Until it is returned our city cannot prosper and the soul of one dear to me cannot rest. Fifty of my friends have sailed with me to claim it. They are the finest men in Greece, all of them sons or grandsons of the immortal gods. This is Telamon, a grandson of Zeus himself. And this is Augeias, the son of Helios the sun-god, and your own half-brother.'

'I have never seen his face before. He is no brother of mine,' King Aietes snapped. 'And who do you claim to be?'

'I am Jason, a kinsman of Phrixus.'

At the name of Phrixus the King's lip quivered with rage. When Phrixus had sought refuge at his court, instead of honouring him as a guest he had murdered him and stolen the Golden Fleece, and he hated being reminded of these crimes.

'Get out of my sight!' he cried, shaking his sceptre in Jason's face. 'You have not come here after a sheep's fleece—you are after my kingdom. Sons and grandsons of the gods, indeed! Do you think I believe that nonsense? You are enemies and traitors. If you stay in my palace another hour, I will tear out your tongues and cut off your hands and send you home with nothing but your feet!'

Telamon was going to answer this outburst defiantly, but Jason checked him and replied with quiet courtesy, 'Sir, please forgive us if our armour makes us look like enemies. I swear we have no designs on your throne. One kingdom is trouble enough—why should we want to burden ourselves with another? It was destiny that brought us here, and the orders of a cruel king. But our claim is just. Give us what we ask, and I will make all Greece ring with your praise.'

These noble words may have moved Medea, but not her father. He stood glaring sullenly at Jason and debating whether to kill him there and then. But he managed to smother his rage and answered cunningly, 'I admit that your claim is just. If you are truly sons of the gods, I will give you the Golden Fleece—on these conditions. Hephaistos once gave me two bulls; they have horns and hooves of bronze, and nostrils that snort fire. You must yoke them together and plough the field of Ares the war-god, where they are now grazing. Next, you must sow the furrows with a serpent's teeth. From these a crop of soldiers will spring up and attack you—you must kill them all . . . Why do you look so downcast? The task is not difficult. I have done it myself, and you are a much younger and stronger man.'

Jason had no choice but to accept and trust to the gods to help him.

'You will start on your task the day after tomorrow in the morning and complete it by sunset,' said King Aietes.

The audience was over and Jason took his leave. As he passed Medea, she lifted her veil and smiled at him. For a moment he gazed in wonder at her face, at her dark beautiful eyes, at the jewels that glittered in her hair like stars. Then he turned away and hurried back to the ship with his two companions.

When Jason reported to the Argonauts he was full of gloom. Peleus at once offered to go in his place, but Jason had accepted the challenge and intended to stand by his promise.

'I am sure Medea would give you any help you asked for,' said Telamon, who had not missed the smile she had given Jason. 'She is so skilled in magic that she can put out a forest fire, dam up torrents, and halt the moon and the stars.'

'Why not meet her in the temple of Hecate?' said Augeias. 'She always goes there at dawn.'

The Argonauts approved, all except Idas, who scoffed, 'Must you look to women to get you out of trouble? You should ask Ares the god of war instead.' But as he always disagreed with everyone they took no notice of his opinion.

There was no need to hide *Argo* in the reeds any longer, so they rowed her upstream and made her fast with hawsers to the jetty. A crowd soon gathered to stare at the handsome strangers. Medea came disguised as one of her maids, with a veil over her face. She had fallen in love with Jason and could not wait to look at him again.

At nightfall the crowd drifted home. Soon the streets were empty, the dogs had stopped barking, and the lights in the sleeping city had been snuffed out.

But Medea could not sleep. She could see the bulls overwhelming Jason in great waves of fire, and the earth army trampling him to death. Could she protect him with her magic drugs without her father knowing? He would kill her if he found out. Yet, as his daughter she owed him loyalty and obedience. Torn between her love for Jason and her feelings for her father, she decided to go to the temple at dawn and ask the goddess what to do.

She lay down on her bed and tried in vain to sleep. She kept running to the window to search the sky— why was the day so long in coming? When at last the stars began to fade she brushed the tangles from her hair, wiped the tears from her cheeks, and put on a long black dress and her loveliest jewellery. Then, with a silver veil over her head and a box of magic ointment in her girdle, she went out.

In the courtyard her carriage was ready. Two maids handed her the reins and whip and stepped in beside her, and off she drove. Her other maids tucked their skirts above their knees and ran along behind, holding on to the wicker back. She did not stop till they had reached the wood where the path to the temple started, by which time her poor maids were quite out of breath, for she had been driving much faster than usual. Stepping down from the carriage, she dismissed them and told them to return for her at noon.

Then she walked unhurriedly along the path under the pine trees, but as soon as her maids were out of sight she broke into a run.

Suddenly she stopped. Jason was standing on the temple steps. She wanted to run into his arms, but could not move. And when he saw her she blushed and did not know where to look.

'Why are you afraid of me?' he said, as he took her trembling hand. 'This is a holy place, and I hope we meet as friends. In the name of Zeus, the protector of strangers, I have come to ask for your help. Without it I could never succeed in the task your father has set me.'

Medea was delighted. She quite forgot that she had come to take her orders from the goddess, and at once gave Jason the magic ointment she had brought.

'Tomorrow at sunrise you must bathe in the river, then melt this ointment and rub it into your skin. Smear some on your armour as well. It is made from the blood-red juice of the yellow crocus and has such power that neither the bulls nor the earth-born army will be able to harm you. But remember this—it can protect you only till sunset.'

'Can it bring me victory, too?' said Jason. 'How is one man alone to kill a whole army?'

'Let them kill themselves,' said Medea. 'Hide yourself, and as soon as the first few soldiers spring up throw a boulder among them. This will turn their fury on themselves and they will fight each other.'

Jason fell on his knees and, thanking her from his heart, swore he would never forget her.

'I wish I could be sure of that,' said Medea. 'Greece is a long way from Colchis.' And as she thought of him sailing off with his prize and leaving her behind, the tears began to trickle down her face. 'If you ever break your word, I shall fly over the seas and plague you like the Harpies.'

They laughed and sat down on the ground and talked together. At midday they were still talking, and by then Jason had already promised Medea nothing less than to take her home with him and make her his bride. He was about to seal his promise with a kiss, when they were startled by a sudden noise of laughter in the bushes. Turning round, they saw Medea's maids peering at them through the leaves and giggling like schoolgirls.

Jason shook his fist at them in mock anger, but Medea felt ashamed before her maids and leapt to her feet.

'I sent you back to the palace,' she said, her eyes flashing.

'You told us to return for you at noon,' they answered pertly. 'It is past noon already.'

'It seems no time at all since I came here,' said Jason.

He would have liked to finish the kiss that the maids had interrupted, but Medea did not think this was the moment for tenderness. She ran after her maids and scolded them all the way back to the carriage. Then she took the whip and reins in her hand and, as the carriage bowled along, tried to think of some way of paying them out. But by the time they reached the palace she had forgotten all about them. She could think of nothing but Jason.

12 THE FIERY BULLS, AND THE SERPENT'S TEETH

Next morning at sunrise Jason bathed in the river, then melted the ointment and rubbed it into his skin from head to foot. When he had smeared it over his armour he asked his friends to test it. They tried to bend his spear, but it was as tough as an iron bar. Refusing to believe it could equal any steel of his, Idas hacked at it with his sword; but the blade rebounded and struck his head. They threw their spears at Jason's shield, but the points buckled. When Pollux the boxer gave him a blow that would have killed an ox Jason only laughed. He waved his shield and shook his spear and leapt into the air, and they all shouted for joy. Then he sent Telamon to King Aietes to fetch the serpent's teeth and tell him he was ready for the fight.

After Telamon's departure, Aietes put on first the breast-plate that the war-god had given him, then his golden helmet—it was as bright as the morning sun when he rises from the stream of Ocean. Grasping his shield and spear, he mounted his chariot and rode out of the town to the field of the war-god. The Argonauts went by river and arrived later, to find him driving up and down impatiently on the bank. All round the field the hills and cliffs of the Caucasus were crowded with people.

As *Argo* touched the bank, Jason leapt ashore. He was stripped to the waist, with his sword slung at his side, and carried his shield and spear and a bronze helmet full of the serpent's teeth. Calmly he watched Aietes step down from his chariot and walk to his throne, where Medea, attended by her maids, was already standing. Between them and himself stretched a sea of mud and grass churned up and trampled by the bulls' hooves, and the bronze yoke and steel plough were lying on the ground. He marched over to the plough, planted his spear in the ground, and put down the helmet. Then he called out in a loud voice that echoed far into the mountains, 'Where are your bulls, Aietes? I am ready.'

From the smoky cave where the bulls slept there was a bellow and they thundered on to the field. Their brazen hooves rang on the ground, their nostrils spurted fire, and they lowered their heads and charged at Jason. Protected by his shield, he was ready for them, firm as a headland in a stormy sea. With a roar the bulls butted the shield, but he did not move. The flames swallowed him, but he was not burnt.

He caught the first bull by the tip of its horn and dragged it to the yoke. With a sudden twist he brought it to its knees. When the second one charged, he dealt with it in the same way. Then he threw aside his shield and held them both down. Castor and Pollux picked up the yoke and handed it to him. He clamped it tight on the bulls' necks and hitched them to the plough, while the two brothers skipped out of the smoke and flame and ran back to the ship. Then he slung his shield across his back and, prodding the bulls forward with his spear, started to plough the field. The bronze share bit into the ground, the earth turned over. The breath from the bulls' nostrils was like a furnace, but in spite of the smoke and swirling flame Jason held the handles steady and did not stumble.

By mid-afternoon the field had been ploughed. A great shout went up from the Argonauts, and there were tears of joy in Medea's eyes. And Jason unyoked the tired bulls and shooed them away.

Then he picked up the helmet and scattered the serpent's teeth right and left, while the earth swallowed them. By the time he had sown the whole field he was hot and sweating, so he ran to the river, dipped his helmet in and quenched his thirst. Glancing over his shoulder, he saw the soil begin to wriggle and crumble—the crop was growing fast. He ran back to the field.

Already spear-points were pushing through like corn; then helmets, heads, shoulders, shields, and fists. An army of soldiers waded out, the soil breaking like waves about their knees; and their armour sparkled in the sunlight like the trembling summer sea. As they

lifted their spears to hurl them at Jason, every Argonaut heart stood still. Medea turned pale. She began to
mutter spells, in case her ointment should not prove
strong enough.

But Jason was not afraid. He picked up a boulder
and hurled it among the soldiers, then quickly
crouched down behind his shield. They could not see

who had thrown it. As Medea had foretold, they sprang upon each other and were felled by their own spears, like pine trees struck down by a gale.

Then Jason drew his sword and threw himself upon them, and while the shadows lengthened over the field he slew them. As fast as fresh soldiers shot up from the earth he cut them down, till they all lay dead on the ground. Then the furrows opened, the earth closed over them, and the sun went down.

And Jason's task was done.

13 THE GOLDEN FLEECE

Aietes had no intention of letting Jason have the Fleece. All night long he sat up with his counsellors planning treachery.

Sickened by the arguing and shouting, Medea retired to her room. She knew that her father would break his word and that he already suspected her of having helped Jason. Unless she escaped with the Argonauts, her life was no longer safe.

She put her magic drugs in a box to take with her, then cut off a lock from her hair and laid it on her pillow for her mother to find. The thought of her mother made her suddenly homesick and hesitant to leave, but she fought against the feeling and ran barefoot from the room and down the empty corridors. The doors were locked, but when she muttered her spells they swung open without a sound. Covering her face with her cloak, she ran through the dark streets and out of the city by a secret way.

At last she came to the river. On the far bank beside a blazing bonfire the Argonauts were celebrating their triumph. She called three times, and Jason recognized her voice and rowed over to her with twelve of his friends.

She clasped him round his knees and begged him to save her from her father. 'Your lives are no safer than mine,' she added. 'We must sail at once.'

'I cannot leave without the Fleece,' said Jason.

'I will take you to it now. But first you must swear to let me come home with you. I have risked my life and everything for you.'

Her pleading moved his heart and again he promised.

Then they took her on board and rowed quickly to the sacred wood, waking the night with the splash of their pine-wood oars. Mooring *Argo* to a tree, they hurried along the path to the grove of the war-god

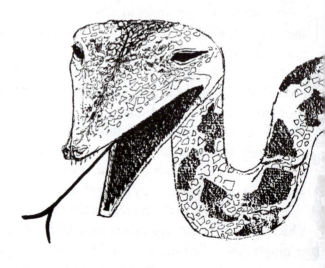

where the Fleece was hanging on an oak tree. They
saw it gleaming in the distance and, when they came
close, they had to shade their eyes.

The serpent lay coiled at the foot of the tree with its head raised; its eyes were flickering like torches. When it saw them coming it stretched out its neck, flashed its forked tongue and hissed. So loud was the hissing that all the leaves in the wood shook. In Colchis babies were startled out of their sleep, and their mothers picked them up from their cradles and hugged them to their breasts.

The loathsome creature slithered forward on its horny scales and opened its huge jaw. It could have swallowed *Argo* and her crew in one gulp.

But Medea walked right up to it and began to stroke its eyelids with a sprig of juniper leaves, which she had already dipped in her ointment. Then she called to Orpheus to sing.

His fingers swept the harp strings in a dreamy tune. He sang of Sleep—the winged god, the child of Night —who stills the waves and the mountain wind and brings rest to god and man and beast. There was not a whisper in the wood.

The cruel jaw sagged. The light in the eyes grew dim as mistletoe. The long coils girdling the tree and twisting far into the darkness beyond relaxed. The hooded eyelids slid down, and the serpent slept.

Then Jason sprang up and seized the Fleece.

As they hurried back through the wood the glow from the Fleece turned Jason's cheeks to fire and the path to liquid gold. They rowed downstream towards the city and at dawn reached the bank where the rest of the Argonauts were waiting.

'The prize is ours,' cried Jason. And as they all cheered he waved the Fleece in the air. But when they tried to grasp it he quickly covered it with his cloak. Then he told them Medea was returning to Greece with them and they must leave at once, before Aietes could stop them.

As soon as they were ready he cut the mooring-rope, then stood beside Medea at the stern. At a word from Ancaeus, the rowers pulled at the oars and *Argo* leapt forward.

Meanwhile Aietes had been gathering his warriors in the market-place. As the ship swept into sight round the river bend they showered her with a hail-storm of arrows. But the Argonauts caught them on their shields and rowed on.

With Aietes at their head, the Colchians streamed along the bank in pursuit. The King, carrying his shield and giant spear, rode in his chariot, while his

young son Apsyrtus whipped on the horses till they were galloping like the wind. But *Argo* had already

reached the sea and was leaping the waves. The chariot nearly went in as well, but Apsyrtus checked the horses just in time. And Aietes stretched out his arms to the sun-god and cried out against Medea and swore revenge.

Three days later the Argonauts anchored at the mouth of the River Halys, where they went ashore to sacrifice and give thanks for their escape. They did not know that Aietes had already launched a fleet and was giving chase. As the smoke from the offering curled up into the sky, the keen-eyed Lyncaeus saw them coming. By the time they had armed themselves and climbed on board, the first ships were an arrow's flight from the shore, barring their outlet to the sea. Their only chance was to try to row straight through them before the rest arrived and the passage was completely blocked.

Seeing a narrow gap between two oncoming banks of oars, Ancaeus steered straight for it. Heaving, straining, tugging, and at the last moment shipping their oars to prevent them being smashed, the Argonauts burst through. The nearer of the two galleys was slower and heavier than *Argo*, and there was a crash of splintering pine-wood as they struck three of the oars. The prow veered round and scraped along her gunwale.

Medea saw her brother Apsyrtus standing in the prow, a flushed and eager stripling, little more than a child. She grabbed him as they passed and dragged him on board—then shouted to the oarsmen to pull clear.

A desperate race began. At first *Argo* seemed to be shaking off her pursuers, but the sea was so cluttered with small islands that she had to dodge and twist, and once she lost her way. Rounding a headland, she saw the galley of Aietes, with the face of the sun-god painted on the sail, swoop down on her.

Then Medea did a terrible thing. Her love for Jason had become a madness; she had to force her father to turn back before he destroyed them both. There was only one way to do this—by killing her brother, for she knew that Aietes would abandon the pursuit till he had buried the boy.

So she killed Apsyrtus and threw his body in pieces into the sea.

The Argonauts were revolted by the crime. But when Jason spoke out against Medea, she cried out passionately, 'I loved my brother, but I killed him because I loved you more. How else could I have saved you?'

This was no answer and, with Orpheus too desolate to sing, there was no music to soothe the pain in Jason's heart. All his friends had turned against Medea, but they would not harm her, because she had given them the Golden Fleece and driven Aietes back.

Then a storm drove them from their course. For many days they were swallowed in mist and darkness and no longer knew where they were. At last the ship was washed up on a shoal, where the waves tipped her over and pounded her with relentless force.

'Goddess Hera,' cried Jason in despair, 'you have been our friend till now. Will you leave us here to drown?'

The goddess answered from the speaking prow, 'Zeus is angry because you killed Apsyrtus, and the sacred ship is stained with his blood. You must suffer for your crime.'

'Medea murdered the boy, not Jason,' the Argonauts

protested. And they seized Medea and would have thrown her into the sea had not Hera stopped them.

'Take your hands off her,' the goddess commanded. 'It is for Zeus to punish her, not you. Besides, you still need her help.'

'Then tell us how we may cleanse ourselves of guilt,' said Jason.

'Only Circe, daughter of the sun-god, can do that for you,' said Hera.

They rammed their oars against the shoal, pushed the ship clear, and went in search of Circe. And while Castor and Pollux prayed to the gods to guide them safely, they rowed hard through the darkness, hoping the brothers' prayer would soon be answered.

But the wildness swallowed them again, and with the sky as wet as the sea they were drenched to the skin. Day after day, night after night, they were tempest-tossed, then driven into scalding waters that sent up clouds of hissing steam. Birds trying to fly overhead brushed against the rigging and fell limp and helpless into the boiling surf. Then they drifted into cooler seas, where for twelve days they were whirled along without seeing sun or stars.

On the thirteenth morning the light of day returned and the sea was calm.

Almost at once the keen-eyed Lyncaeus sighted land—dark cliffs crowned with trees, and a beach of silver sand.

'It is the island of Circe, my father's sister,' said Medea.

Ancaeus steered for the shore, and soon they saw a woman standing knee-deep in the water, washing

her hair. On the shore was a flock of weird-limbed creatures that looked like neither men nor beasts. As the ship drew near they barked and whined and bleated and, when the heroes landed, scampered into the wood. The woman stood and waited on the sand.

Medea recognized her as Circe and greeted her shyly; but Circe, though she knew Medea and seemed to be expecting her, gave no greeting in return.

'Where is your brother Apsyrtus?' she said.

'What do you know of him?' Medea cried.

'Last night I dreamed that the walls of my house were streaming with blood, your brother's blood. It was you who shed it.' She looked at the sword which had killed Apsyrtus and which now hung at Jason's side. 'What do you want from me?'

'To be cleansed of our guilt,' said Medea.

'Come into the house,' said Circe, and she beckoned to the Argonauts to follow.

But Jason told them curtly to stay outside. He had been watching Circe's beasts as they slunk between the trees, with their cowed looks and shifty eyes. He did not trust her, for he knew they had been men when they came to Circe's island. So he went into the house with Medea alone.

A room with wide windows overlooked the sea, and here by the hearth the two suppliants knelt down. But Circe made them sit on her polished chairs and face her, while she lashed them with her tongue for the cruel deed—till Medea cried out to her to stop.

Then Circe led them into the courtyard, where she killed a sucking pig and sprinkled their hands with its blood. Calling on Zeus to forgive them, she turned to her weeping niece and, with a touch of pity, said, 'You are marrying this stranger against your father's will and sailing to a home you know nothing about. Such disobedience is wrong, I cannot excuse it. But as you are both my suppliant and my niece, I will not add further to your misery. Take food and wine for the ship, and leave my house.'

Medea sobbed as if her heart would break. She forgot about the food and wine and, covering her eyes with her scarf, grabbed Jason's cold and trembling hand and ran from the house, down to the waiting ship.

16 THE MUSIC OF THE SIRENS

The goddess Hera sent them fair winds from the west, and some days later they sighted a small rocky island. From across the water came the sound of music, which to the tired Argonauts was refreshing beyond words and lured them on.

But Medea sternly warned them to keep away. 'Three sea nymphs, called Sirens, live here,' she told them. 'They watch out all day long for ships and use their music to tempt sailors ashore and destroy them.'

Already they could see the nymphs. They were sitting on the rocks, one playing the flute, another the lyre, while the third was singing a dreamy song and stretching out her arms towards them. The fish in the sea, the gulls in their nests, and the lazy seals basking on the sand were all listening entranced.

The heroes closed their eyes; their heads nodded on their chests; the oars slipped from their hands. Caught in the current, the ship drifted slowly towards the shore.

But Medea could see human bones littering the beach, skulls with empty sockets staring from the shallows. She tried in vain to rouse the Argonauts—her shouts and warnings had no effect.

She remembered Orpheus, the champion of all singers, enchanting all who heard him—man and bird and beast. Even trees marched to his song, and

when it ended they shed their leaves like tears. And she cried out to him, 'Can the Sirens' music be more powerful than yours? Can you not drown their song?'

Then Orpheus played a rollicking sailors' tune. It roused the Argonauts from their stupor. Hands began to clap, feet to drum on the deck, and heads to wag from side to side in rhythm. The gulls rose from their nests and circled above the mast-head. The seals slithered into the sea and chased each other; horny crabs patter-danced on the rocks.

Then Jason called on the Argonauts to pull away from the island; and Ancaeus the helmsman headed out to sea. As the oars struck together and the shore slowly receded, the music of the Sirens became a fading dream.

For all except Butes, an oarsman in the bows. He was leaning over the side, straining to listen, longing to reach the outstretched arms. Before anyone could stop him, he jumped overboard and lashed out for the shore.

As the ship drew out to sea the voice of Orpheus echoed from the cliffs more faintly. But the music of the Sirens swelled and hummed till all the air was throbbing. Butes could hear nothing else, and on and on across the red path of the sunset he swam. He fought through the surf, scattering the seals before him. He splashed ashore and lay panting on the sand.

'Sirens, I am sick to death of wandering, of fighting wind and storm,' he cried. 'Let me stay with you for ever. Let me listen to your song and rest.'

On the rocks above the three nymphs stopped their singing and peered down at him with gloating eyes. They laid down the lute and lyre and with slow and cruel steps began to walk towards him.

Butes was afraid. He saw that the sand, which from the ship had looked so clean and sparkling, was white with bones. They had been living limbs till the Sirens had done with them and the tide had picked them clean. He tried to run back into the sea.

The Sirens sprang at him. Their fingers fastened on his arms like eagles' claws.

But far away on the peak of Mount Ida, Aphrodite, the goddess of love, had been watching and had pitied his distress. She swooped down and snatched him from their grasp, then flew away with him back to her mountain home. As she whirled through the air, the fires of the sunset turned her wings to red and gold. The wailing of the Sirens died away, and soon the rocky island was only a speck in the sea.

17 THE WEDDING

The Argonauts sailed on.

Passing Mount Etna, they came to the monster rock of Scylla, a place of screaming spray and booming seas, hollow with caves. As they tried to steer past, the whirlpool of Charybdis caught them and spun them round, sucking them lower and lower as they neared the centre, till the mast-head was level with the rim of the pool. The rowers tugged at their oars, Ancaeus leaned hard on the helm, but they could not break away.

Then Ancaeus saw a head in their wake—Thetis, Queen of the sea, swimming to help them. She laid her guiding hand on the blade of the steering-oar, and from all round the ship her sea-nymphs sprang up, dancing on the waves like dolphins. They touched the ship and passed her from hand to hand till she was clear of the whirling water. When the rock threatened to smash her to pieces they ran along the reef to fend her off, then waved their white arms to the Argonauts and dived to their kingdom below.

A week later the Argonauts came to an island walled round with cliffs and, finding a harbour, rowed boldly in to ask for food and water. It was the island of King Alcinous, who welcomed them with open arms.

But they had hardly stepped ashore when a boat-load of armed Colchians put in. They had come from the Black Sea in pursuit of *Argo* and now angrily demanded the return of Medea to her father. Alcinous ruled that the claims of a husband came before those of a father. He said that if Jason and Medea were married at once, instead of waiting till their return to Iolcos as they had planned, he would send the Colchians away.

This was glad news, and that night the wedding

was celebrated in a sacred cave by the shore. The nymphs of the goddess Hera came with their arms heaped with flowers. As they scattered them round the Fleece, which had been spread over a bed, the radiance from the wool danced in their eyes like flames reflected from a fire. They took Jason and his bride to the bed, then stood at the mouth of the cave with the heroes, while Orpheus led the wedding song with his lyre, beating time with his foot. Everyone joined in the singing, while a few guards stood by in case of surprise attack.

But they need not have been afraid, for the fleet of Alcinous was drawn up in line beyond the cliff; and as soon as Jason and Medea were man and wife the Colchians were ordered to leave the harbour. The wedding song drowned their shouting and the angry splash of their oars as they crossed the moonlit bay. Then gradually the voices faded, and Orpheus ended his song:

> 'Love, be not brief
> As the halcyon summer,
> Wither not as the winter leaf,
> But like the enchanted floating nest
> Bring to the wind-flecked breakers rest,
> And calm the storm.'

It was the poet's prayer for the lovers, for though he feared for their love he longed for their happiness.

In the cave Jason was listening. And he remembered the two lovers whom the gods had changed into kingfishers to save them from despair, and how each winter for seven clear days their nest floated on the summer-quiet sea. In his thoughts the Golden Fleece turned now into the floating nest. But round it the waves were raging and would not be stilled.

Crowds flocked to the harbour to see the Argonauts depart, while Alcinous brought wedding gifts and everything they needed for the voyage back to Greece. Then they rowed to the harbour mouth, hoisted the sail and raced before the wind.

But the fine weather did not l⌐⌐ A nine-day gale swept them south towards Africa, into a gulf full of islands of floating seaweed, with sandbanks and shoals everywhere.

One morning they woke to find themselves keel-dry on the sand. The sea had vanished and the African desert lay all round them, a lifeless world without hills or trees or anything green at all. Ancaeus the helmsman was in despair, and Idas was quick to blame him for their plight.

All day the pitiless sun beat down, and night with its cooling shadows was long in coming. Exhausted and dreading the return of day, they lay down on the sand to sleep.

Then the goddess Hera appeared to Jason while he slept. With gentle fingers she lifted the cloak that covered his head.

'Do not despair, Jason,' she said. 'Your courage has

won you the Golden Fleece and carried
you safely over half the world. Tomorrow Poseidon
the sea-god will send you a sign. You must follow
it, and will return safely home.'

He opened his eyes and leapt to his feet to question
her further. But she had vanished, and all he saw was
the dawn chasing the darkness from the sky.

Waking his friends, he told them of his dream, and
while the water crept slowly back over the shallows
they tried to puzzle out its meaning.

Suddenly a monster horse bounded out of the sea,
tossing the spray from its golden mane, then galloped
straight past them over the sand.

Idas was for launching the ship at once, but Peleus thought this a foolish plan. 'We would drift on to the shoals again and be at the mercy of the first storm,' he said. 'The galloping horse was one of Poseidon's team and we must follow its tracks.'

'Too much sun has made you mad,' said Idas. 'How can we sail across the desert?'

'We can carry the ship on our shoulders,' said Peleus.

'Peleus is right,' said Jason. 'Poseidon has sent us his sign, and the hoofprints will lead us to deep water where we can launch the ship safely.'

So they hoisted *Argo* on to their shoulders and for twelve days and nights, sweating and straining, tormented with thirst, carried her over the burning sand. Two of the heroes died on the way—Canthus first, then Mopsus the prophet, who was bitten by a snake.

At last the hoofprints brought them to a lagoon, and they waded in and set their burden down. When they had drunk from a stream nearby, they went on board, stepped the mast and unfurled the sail. In the folds and creases they found many scorpions, which they threw at Idas as a joke—he had shirked his share of the carrying and never stopped grumbling.

Ancaeus quickly found the way to the open sea, and soon they were scudding over the waves towards Crete, with the south wind at their backs.

They decided to land in Crete for food and water.

As they were sailing along below the cliffs looking for an opening, suddenly a huge lump of rock splashed into the sea beside them. A column of water shot up into the air and as it fell back swept the rowers from their benches and half swamped the ship.

Jason looked up to see where the rock had come from. Towering on the cliff-top he saw a giant of bronze; and the sun's reflection blazed from every yard of his body, dazzling their eyes. Realizing that the rock had not fallen by accident, he ordered the crew to back water before the giant threw another at them.

Scrambling to the benches, the rowers tugged at the oars, and they were soon out of range. They would have sailed right away, but Medea asked Jason to turn back.

'We need food and water badly. Why should we let this giant bully us?' she said. And she told them that his name was Talos and that Hephaistos the fire-god had forged him out of bronze and given him to King Minos of Crete to guard the island. His habit was to walk right round the island three times a day, and if any strangers tried to land he leapt into his furnace in the hills, then rushed out on them red-hot and burnt them up.

'What chance have we against a man of fire?' said Idas sulkily. 'Let us put out to sea before he scorches us to death.'

'He is as mortal as you are,' said Medea. 'I know his secret and can master him.'

She told them he had been made with a single vein, filled with liquid fire and stoppered above one ankle with a bronze nail. If the nail was pulled out, his life blood would flow away and he would die.

While they were talking, Talos was standing on the cliff, smoky with anger. As they were out of range of his rocks, he began to hurl abuse at them instead.

As soon as he paused for breath, Medea answered him over the water, coaxingly, with honeyed words. 'Noble Talos, I am Medea the enchantress. I heard your name on the other side of the world. But even men of brass must die and be forgotten. Do you want to be like the gods and live for ever?'

'Live for ever?' echoed the cliffs.

She held up a crystal cup and said, 'Here I have immortal blood. Circe, my father's sister, gave it to me to bring to you, to honour you for your greatness. Noble Talos, shall I pour it into your veins? Do you want to live for ever?'

'Live for ever?' echoed the cliffs.

As Talos tilted down his head to look into the cup a ray of light reflected from his body touched the crystal and made it glow. For all his brazen strength, he was simple-minded—as many giants are—and believed Medea's words. Impatient to be made a god, he beckoned to her with flashing arms to bring the cup ashore.

Ancaeus steered into a sheltered cove. Then Jason lifted Medea down on to the beach.

With a clanking sound the giant stooped and stretched his huge length along the cliff-top, singeing the turf wherever his body touched. He lowered his leg over the edge till his toes were scraping the beach. The heat from his foot was like the glow of a furnace, and the air in the cove was sick with fumes.

Medea had to act quickly before she choked. Her nimble fingers found the nail above the ankle and pulled it out. But she did not pour her precious liquid in—it was only sea water and would not have been much use. Instead she let the giant's blood leak out, oozing over the rocks like a stream of molten lava, down to the hissing sea.

At once a heavy drowsiness overcame Talos, and at first he welcomed it, for he thought it part of the treatment. When he saw Medea skipping over the rocks towards the ship he became suspicious and tried to lever himself up. But he was too feeble; half his life-blood was already spilt. He fell back with a cry, his metal eyelids snapped shut, and slowly his bronze flesh turned green.

Jason and Medea clambered on board, and the ship pulled clear of the surf, already boiling with the giant's blood. Her sail set, *Argo* was half across the bay when, with a gasp like the puff from a volcano, Talos died; and his body clattered over the cliff edge and crashed to the rocks below.

Then the Argonauts remembered they had taken no food or water on board, so they had to sail back again. But they were careful to avoid the stretch of coast where Talos lay.

20 THE END OF THE VOYAGE

The wind held and, after watering the ship at Aegina, they rounded Cape Sunium and sailed home up the long Euboean coast. For the last stretch of the voyage Orpheus stood at the prow with his harp and sang of the joy they felt at coming home. As they sighted the top of Mount Pelion and the cliffs of Iolcos they shook off their weariness and their spirits soared. And Orpheus sang:

'O cliffs of home, mountains and fields and trees,
  How many years since we did part!
You reach your hands out over the tired seas
  And touch my heart.'

But no welcome awaited them. As they rowed into the harbour the only answer to their merry shouts and waving hands was puzzled, stony looks. Who were these foreigners with the wild beards and dark leathery skins? And the ship, with her blistered paint, battered timbers and torn sail—where did she come from?

As the Argonauts stepped ashore a crowd gathered round them, and Jason explained who they were and where they had been all these years.

An old man came forward. He looked searchingly at him and said, 'I saw Jason once, long ago. His eyes were like stars on a frosty night, and he walked like a god. You are not he.'

Then Jason took Medea to the palace, where they found his uncle, King Pelias, now old and crippled. He did not believe their tale either and said the Argonauts had been drowned years before.

Jason's mother was dead. But his father Aeson was still alive, and they found him lying in a room nearby, blind and too frail to leave his bed. Kneeling at his feet, he took the old man's hands in his and kissed them. He told him of his wedding to Medea and of how she had helped him to win the Golden Fleece; so the soul of their kinsman Phrixus could rest at last and their city prosper.

Aeson recognized his voice and, welcoming Medea, too, cried out joyfully, 'I thank the gods for answering my prayers. Do not leave me again, my son. You shall live here in the palace with your wife, for the throne is now yours by right.'

There were feasts and thank-offerings to celebrate the safe return. Bulls with golden horns were sacrificed to the gods and incense heaped high on the altar flames. And the Golden Fleece was displayed for everyone to see.

But Aeson was too ill to take part in these rejoicings. In pity for him, Jason took Medea aside and said, 'Dearest wife, I owe to you my safety, my happiness and all my triumphs. Can you do one thing more for me? Can you take away some of my own years of life and give them to my father?'

Medea was touched by her husband's love for Aeson, for she had not forgotten how she had deserted her own father. But she did not think it right to cut short Jason's life, even if she were able to.

'With the help of Hecate, goddess of witchcraft, whom I serve, I will do something even better,' she said. 'I will try to make your father young again.'

On the night of the full moon she went into the woods alone. Kneeling down, she stretched out her arms to the stars and prayed to the goddess to help her.

Suddenly her dragon chariot appeared. She climbed in and flew away to the plains of Thessaly, where she spent nine days and nights gathering the herbs she needed to make her brew of youth. When it was ready she returned to Iolcos, emptied the blood out of Aeson's veins and poured in the juice of her herbs. At once he lost his pale and scraggy looks; his grey hair and beard turned black; his wrinkles vanished. He was a young man again.

When they saw this astonishing change the daughters of Pelias naturally wanted the same treatment for their own father. But Medea resented the wrongs he had done to Jason's family and was angry at his reluctance to give him the kingdom as he had promised. Pretending to help his daughters, she mixed a different brew, and Pelias was killed.

The people of Iolcos were appalled, and so was Jason. The cruel murder of his uncle was to ruin him as well as Medea. Forced to leave the country, they fled to Corinth.

In the ten years they lived there several children were born to them. But Medea's nature grew increasingly savage and gloomy, and Jason's love for her withered and died. He deserted her and asked the King of Corinth if he might marry his daughter Glauce. But Medea murdered her on the very day she was to have married him. To spite him further, she killed two of her own children, too, then escaped in her dragon chariot and vanished for ever from Jason's life.

With no kingdom of his own, and no wife to make him happy, his remaining years were lonely and sad. The Argonauts had all scattered; and Orpheus, whom he had loved deeply and whose song had always cheered him, he never saw again. He wandered from city to city, rejected and humiliated wherever he went. Finally, in his old age he returned to Corinth, where long ago he had beached *Argo* and left her on the shore as a monument dedicated to the gods.

One day he was sitting in the shadow of the prow, thinking of the great deeds of the past. By now some of the ship's timbers had rotted, and a beam from the prow fell on his head and killed him.

After his death, Poseidon the sea-god placed an image of *Argo* among the stars to shine there for ever. So Jason's greatness was not forgotten.

What's in a myth?

The story of Jason, like many myths, is thousands of years old.
Myths were first told by storytellers and were not written down
until much later.

When these stories were first told, events in the world were
explained as the work of gods and goddesses who lived on
Mount Olympus. When a wind suddenly sprang up it was
because the god in charge of the wind had let it out of its bag.
Day turned into night because the horses which pulled the sun
god's chariot across the sky were tired and needed rest. Some
humans who seemed to be extra clever or brave were thought
to have a god as one of their parents. The gods and goddesses
would help people to fight storms, monsters and magic. But
these same gods and goddesses could also become angry and
spiteful.

These myths were set in real places and it is still possible to visit
many of them. On their way home, the Argonauts stopped for a
break at Aegina and rounded Cape Sunium (see p92). The
Island of Aegina is a short ferry trip from Piraeus, the port of
Athens. You can go up through pistachio groves to the ruined
temple at the top of the hill. Cape Sunium, with its views out
to the islands, is also easily reached from Athens. It has the
remains of a striking temple to Poseidon, the god of the sea.

Many of the characters in *The Clashing Rocks*, gods and humans,
also appear in other stories. *The Way of Danger* is also by Ian
Serraillier and can be found in the New Windmill Series. In
that book you can read more about Medea, the beautiful but
wicked witch, and you can discover more about King Minos
and the dangers lurking in his kingdom of Crete.

Who's who

In the story of Jason you hear about many people whom you may wish to look up quickly. The list below gives a brief description of some of them. The first page number is the page where the character first appears. The second page number shows where there is a more complete story about a character who may appear only once or twice.

Aeson forced from the throne of Iolcos by his half-brother Pelias. He was Jason's father, and was afraid Pelias might kill Jason (p3)

Aietes King of Colchis. He had stolen the Golden Fleece from Phrixus (pp12, 45)

Amazons race of women warriors (p41)

Apollo handsome god of the sun, journeys, music and poetry (p10)

Apsyrtus Medea's young half-brother, killed by her (p45)

Ares god of war (p10). His Latin name is Mars

Argo name of Jason's ship (p14)

Argonauts men who sailed with Jason (p15)

Argus shipbuilder who gave his name to the *Argo* (p14)

Athene city-goddess of Athens, very wise (p18)

Chiron a centaur. Centaurs had the head, chest and arms of a man, but the four legs and body of a horse. They were wise, gentle and gifted, but if they got drunk they behaved badly (p1)

Circe Aietes' sister, Medea's aunt. She had magic powers and turned men into pigs (p71)

Hades god of the Underworld, brother of Zeus and Poseidon. The name is also used for the Underworld itself – a gloomy place where the souls of the dead wander (p41)

Harpies monsters with a woman's face and body and a bird's wings and claws. The word means 'snatchers' (p30)

Hecate	goddess of witchcraft (p45)
Hephaistos	god of fire and blacksmith to the gods (p45). His Latin name is Vulcan
Hera	a goddess, the wife of Zeus, chief of the gods (p8)
Heracles	a giant of a man, very strong and clever (p4). His Latin name is Hercules
Hylas	Heracles' page, who disappeared (pp15, 26)
Jason	sent as a young child, by Aeson his father, to Chiron, to be brought up. Becomes Captain of the *Argo* (p3)
Medea	King Aietes' daughter, a beautiful but wicked witch who fell in love with Jason and helped him (p45)
Minos	King of the island of Crete (p87)
Nymphs	beautiful creatures, seen as young women, with some of the powers of gods and goddesses. They lived in the sea, rivers, lakes, fountains, trees, hills and woods (p3)
Orpheus	poet and musician whose songs and music could calm people, and tame birds, animals and fish (p15)
Phrixus	original owner of the Golden Fleece, kinsman of Jason, murdered by Aietes (p12)
Poseidon	brother of Zeus and god of the sea (p24). His Latin name is Neptune
Prometheus	a Titan, who made the first man out of clay and stole the gods' fire to give to humans. For this he was severely punished by Zeus (p44)
Sirens	three sea-nymphs whose singing made sailors want to land on their island. If they did, the Sirens killed them (p45)
Talos	giant of bronze, made by Hephaistos to guard the island of Crete (p87)
Titans	the older generation of gods, before the Olympian gods, the children of Uranus (heaven) and Gaia (Earth)
Zeus	the chief of the gods (p8). His Latin name is Jupiter

Pronunciation guide

You may wish to use the list below to help you to pronounce some of the names in the story. It uses the 'say' method of the *Heinemann English Dictionary*.

The letter 'i' should be pronounced as 'i' in 'hit'.
The letter 'o' between consonants should be pronounced as 'o' in 'pot'.
'th' should be pronounced as in 'thin'.
The single apostrophe (') is called a schwa. It should be pronounced like the first 'a' in 'banana'.

Acheron	**a** - k'ron	**Cyzicus**	**si** - zi - k's
Aeneas	i - **nee** - 's	**Hecate**	**hek** - a - tee
Aeson	**ee** - s'n	**Helle**	**hell** - i
Aietes	ee - **ee** - tees	**Hephaistos**	heff - **ee** - st'ss
Alcimede	al - sim - **ee** - dee	**Hera**	**hee** - ra
		Heracles	**herra** - kleez
Ancaeus	an - **see** - us	**Medea**	mid - **ee** - a
Aphrodite	aff - roe - **die** - tee	**Minos**	**mie** - noss
		Orpheus	**awe** - feeus
Athene	ath - **ee** - nee	**Phrixus**	**frik** - s's
Augeias	awe - **gee** - 's	**Polyphemus**	polly - **fee** - m's
Charybdis	k'**rib** - diss		
Chiron	**kie** - r'n	**Poseidon**	poss - **ie** - d'n
Circe	**sir** - see	**Scylla**	**sill** - a
Colchis	**kol** - kiss	**Tiphys**	**tif** - iss

ALSO IN

Founding Editors: Anne and Ian Serraillier

Chinua Achebe Things Fall Apart
Vivien Alcock The Cuckoo Sister; The Monster Garden;
The Trial of Anna Cotman; A Kind of Thief; Ghostly Companions
Margaret Atwood The Handmaid's Tale
Jane Austen Pride and Prejudice
J G Ballard Empire of the Sun
Nina Bawden The Witch's Daughter; A Handful of Thieves; Carrie's
War; The Robbers; Devil by the Sea; Kept in the Dark; The Finding;
Keeping Henry; Humbug; The Outside Child
Valerie Bierman No More School
Melvin Burgess An Angel for May
Ray Bradbury The Golden Apples of the Sun; The Illustrated Man
Betsy Byars The Midnight Fox; Goodbye, Chicken Little; The
Pinballs; The Not-Just-Anybody Family; The Eighteenth Emergency
Victor Canning The Runaways; Flight of the Grey Goose
Ann Coburn Welcome to the Real World
Hannah Cole Bring in the Spring
Jane Leslie Conly Racso and the Rats of NIMH
Robert Cormier We All Fall Down; Tunes for Bears to Dance to
Roald Dahl Danny, The Champion of the World; The Wonderful
Story of Henry Sugar; George's Marvellous Medicine; The BFG;
The Witches; Boy; Going Solo; Matilda
Anita Desai The Village by the Sea
Charles Dickens A Christmas Carol; Great Expectations;
Hard Times; Oliver Twist; A Charles Dickens Selection
Peter Dickinson Merlin Dreams
Berlie Doherty Granny was a Buffer Girl; Street Child
Roddy Doyle Paddy Clarke Ha Ha Ha
Gerald Durrell My Family and Other Animals
Anne Fine The Granny Project
Anne Frank The Diary of Anne Frank
Leon Garfield Six Apprentices; Six Shakespeare Stories;
Six More Shakespeare Stories
Jamila Gavin The Wheel of Surya
Adele Geras Snapshots of Paradise

Alan Gibbons Chicken
Graham Greene The Third Man and The Fallen Idol; Brighton Rock
Thomas Hardy The Withered Arm and Other Wessex Tales
L P Hartley The Go-Between
Ernest Hemmingway The Old Man and the Sea; A Farewell to Arms
Nigel Hinton Getting Free; Buddy; Buddy's Song
Anne Holm I Am David
Janni Howker Badger on the Barge; Isaac Campion; Martin Farrell
Jennifer Johnston Shadows on Our Skin
Toeckey Jones Go Well, Stay Well
Geraldine Kaye Comfort Herself; A Breath of Fresh Air
Clive King Me and My Million
Dick King-Smith The Sheep-Pig
Daniel Keyes Flowers for Algernon
Elizabeth Laird Red Sky in the Morning; Kiss the Dust
D H Lawrence The Fox and The Virgin and the Gypsy;
Selected Tales
Harper Lee To Kill a Mockingbird
Ursula Le Guin A Wizard of Earthsea
Julius Lester Basketball Game
C Day Lewis The Otterbury Incident
David Line Run for Your Life
Joan Lingard Across the Barricades; Into Exile; The Clearance;
The File on Fraulein Berg
Robin Lister The Odyssey
Penelope Lively The Ghost of Thomas Kempe
Jack London The Call of the Wild; White Fang
Bernard Mac Laverty Cal; The Best of Bernard Mac Laverty
Margaret Mahy The Haunting
Jan Mark Do You Read Me? (Eight Short Stories)
James Vance Marshall Walkabout
W Somerset Maugham The Kite and Other Stories
Ian McEwan The Daydreamer; A Child in Time
Pat Moon The Spying Game
Michael Morpurgo Waiting for Anya; My Friend Walter;
The War of Jenkins' Ear
Bill Naughton The Goalkeeper's Revenge
New Windmill A Charles Dickens Selection
New Windmill Book of Classic Short Stories
New Windmill Book of Nineteenth Century Short Stories

How many have you read?